THE
PUPPY
PROPHET

Praise for The Puppy Prophet

With each page, Lane beautifully portrays the unguarded and unconditional love our dogs offer, encouraging us to open our hearts just as they do. The Puppy Prophet will undoubtedly become a sweet companion for anyone who shares a bond with a dog. The book is a heart-touching journey, where the love and wisdom of dogs illuminate the path to living in the now. Whether you are a dog lover or not, The Puppy Prophet will leave a lasting imprint on your heart and soul, inspiring you to embrace simple joys and profound teachings.
Christopher L. Heuertz, Author of The Sacred Enneagram and The Enneagram of Belonging

David Cary Lane is a thoughtful and poignant writer who invites you to grow and laugh and feel through honest yet playful words of wisdom. Dog lover or not, The Puppy Prophet will give you joy to read.
Jonathan Merritt, Author of Learning to Speak God from Scratch and contributor for The Atlantic

The timeless truths and inspirational poems of The Puppy Prophet will stay with you long after you close the book. Your heart will be lifted, and your imagination ignited as you savor each poem and linger over every page. David Cary Lane is a gifted storyteller and poet whose words invite you to paws and ponder the beautiful lessons our canine friends have to teach us. I highly recommend this book!
Jennifer Marshall Bleakley, Best-Selling Author of the Pawverbs book series

One of the great gifts of poetry is the invitation to reorient ourselves to the world around us by way of language. What I loved about The Puppy Prophet is the way David Cary Lane invites us to reorient our hearts toward levity and the kind of meaningful connection available when we are softer (with ourselves and one another). This work isn't simply "sweet" though there is a sweetness to it. This work has the weight of sincere humanity.
Justin McRoberts, Author of Sacred Strides: The Journey to Belovedness in Work and Rest

From a world without peanut butter to friendship, beauty, and mystery, come along as Daisy, who loves the sun but cares for the clouds, too, shares the gentle wisdom she's gained from years of experiencing the quirks of both humans and her fellow canines. A short book, but don't do it the injustice of making it a quick read. Savor your moments with Daisy—you'll find them time well-spent.
Tom Allen, Author of Grace Happens: Adventures in Everyday Living

A brilliant book full of wisdom and hope. As I read, I couldn't keep myself from smiling, nodding along, and even tearing up. What a gift this book will be to so many.
Tanner Olson, Author of As You Go and Walk a Little Slower, Poet, and dad to Pancake the Goldendoodle

If you're looking for a cheerful, applicable read with deep meaning for yourself or your kids before bed, I highly recommend The Puppy Prophet. These simple yet elegant poems remind us of God's love for us, and how he meets us always with love and grace.
Pat Brown, CEO at Surv

David the human and Daisy the dog so gently and warmly welcome and guide us back home. Not home to where the peanut butter and pup treats reside, but home to ourselves, where belovedness and belonging are unquestionably known. What a gift this book is to our weary souls.
Tyler Hill, Spiritual Director and Author

In a delightful and concise format, Daisy the dumpster dog imparts wisdom and radiates enlightenment within her canine circle. Through her brief yet impactful exhortations, she guides her fellow dogs on a transformative journey, highlighting the profound influence of courage, love, kindness, and leadership in their lives. And in this heartfelt tale, her wisdom effortlessly transcends to resonate with us humans, leaving a lasting impression.
Randal Ford, Photographer and creator of Good Dog

Christ has 10,000 faces, and in The Puppy Prophet, it looks like Dumpster Daisy. Stories are sneaky. They neutralize our normal defense mechanisms and travel deep enough to knock on the hidden doors of our soul. This is exactly what Lane's writing does in this fun and beautiful book. If you wonder, how can one ask our most pressing personal and cosmic questions through an eclectic group of fictional dogs? Well, you should find out by reading The Puppy Prophet.
Kevin Sweeney, Spiritual Director, Author of The Making of a Mystic and The Joy of Letting Go, and host of The Church Needs Therapy podcast

THE
PUPPY
PROPHET

DAVID CARY LANE

Illustrated by
Patrick Atkins

Foreword by
Levi The Poet

To all the dogs in all the houses
who make those walls a home.

Contents

Foreword

My dog, Francis (or, St. Frank — if you will — named after the Patron Saint of Animals, himself), is the curliest thirty-five-pound bundle of soul you've never met. He was born a dark merlot, but — three short, long years later — transformed into a gray that keeps begging peoples' question, "My god, man, how'd you stress your dog out so bad?"

He's just empathetic, I think.

One time, in Santa Barbara, California, we were together walking the shoreline left of Hendry's Beach, and the singer in my ears chiseled language into some dam I didn't know existed inside of me, and I quivered against the sea wall, and Frank's playfulness morphed into protectiveness. He built a kind of invisible perimeter around the puddle I became — some center whose lap he'd sit on with cheeks to lick clean before barking away the other passersby infringing upon our borders.

He's got Spirit in his eyes, and I know the cartoons were true, no matter what my theology teachers said: all dogs do go to heaven. Or... that's not quite right. It's something more like, "All dogs reveal heaven, here."

In the words of Daisy, The Puppy Prophet herself: "Grace abounds here and now, breathe it in — savor This."

And when I watch my dog — tree that he is, just being himself, freaking out at every shadow in the park — I believe Daisy when she says, "It's not how loud you bark, or how well you behave — it's seizing the scandal of grace by seizing the freedom to play."

I've been reading John O'Donohue's Anam Cara as of late, so the language of Soul Friends bookends the shelf inside of my chest where every one of these dogs sits — longings and insecurities and dreams and contradictions and terrors and envies and delights and sadness and happiness and cowardice and courage and the goodbyes I've wept that are always deaths before I'm alive again.

And just like the glimpses I keep catching in St. Frank's sideways glances, Dumpster Daisy is alive in all of them.

I wish you all the play in the world.

Levi The Poet

Humans called her

Dumpster Daisy

She was a shabby old mutt; dirt coated her nails, fog clouded her eyes, twigs clung to her fur.

Scruffy yet elegant, wild yet composed, she was a gray-haired stray with a different kind of home.

Daisy spent her days as most strays do, wandering and resting. She'd follow a scent, she'd comfort a stranger, she'd lay in the grass cloaked by the symptoms of the sun.

Daisy loved the sun, but she cared for the clouds too.

Every evening, just before her sun bid the day farewell, Daisy meandered over to the park. She'd watch the other dogs bounding about, dragging their humans out of hiding, drooling for freedom.

The dogs would frantically fetch and rigorously wrestle, they'd whizz through the water and tinkle on the trees, chase children and dart after ducks.

A splendorous spectacle to behold.

Daisy observed on a hill from afar, feelings of fondness filled her ribcage as her jaded joints kept her still.

But on one particularly brisk, fall day, the breeze drew Daisy down
to the magnolia tree in the middle of the park. Its branches extended
endlessly, its shade a shared shelter.

Daisy sat upright, closed her eyes, and lifted her snout, as if to sniff a
shifting in the winds.

Her time had come.

Steady and serene, Daisy breathed gently, in and out, with an
alluring confidence.

The other dogs took notice; her presence was palpable, her spirit
inviting. Slowly they gathered around, compelled by their curiosity,
welcomed by her warmth.

Then Daisy did something dogs rarely do; she spoke. Her bark was both bold and gentle, hypnotically captivating.

My fellow furry friends,
I've lived more lives than any dog need endure.

I've toiled the lengthy leash and walked the endless streets,
Minded the brilliance of birds and silly squirrels beneath.

Patrolled the windows, guarded the castle.
Fetched the balls despite the hassle.

Gnawed the gnarliest of bones in all the land
And lost my dear human to time's heartless hand.

Yes, I've bore all the weights and ecstasies under the sun,
Yet with each passing moon, more a puppy I've become.

What have I gained but the wisdom I may share?
What have I lost but the time that has brought me here?

Your souls inclined you to gather around.
So, take heart, hear thy call, and ask me now . . .

I know not all, but with this pure admission alone,
You may trust the words which pour from my seasoned soul.

Accolades and praise are not my aim, for my time here draws nigh.
But with my final panting, I hope that I might bark wisdom's cry.

A deafening moment of silence followed her words. All the dogs precariously sat, vigilantly uncertain, shifting their eyes and cocking their heads.

Poncho

The pudgy Pug

Among the pack was Poncho, the pudgy Pug. He was a bashful little pup, known more for his blubber than for his bravery. But here, in this moment, a tingle of courage rippled through his wrinkles. He waddled forward and found himself, almost unconsciously, breaking the quiet of the crowd with a question:

Why does the peanut butter always run out?
Why can I not have an eternal reservoir on my snout?

Daisy smiled empathetically. She herself had longed for an answer to such a question in the past, although cookies were more her fancy. She responded:

More, more, more, there will always be more.
Slyly lying in such hope, presence is presently torn.

Can taste be savored if the mouth forever seeks its next victim?
Can longing be quenched through thirst's repetitious rhythm?

A generous gift in proper proportion is truer whole,
While the curse of abundance rots even a grateful soul.

What you have, you have; what you will, you will.
Dare I say, a peanut butter-less world is yet a world still.

Having wished Daisy would offer a map with directions to an extensive stash of his favorite brown sugary goo, Poncho was a tad frustrated. He fell back into the ranks of the other dogs, pondering a world without.

Dennis

The doubting Doberman

Dennis, the doubting Doberman, stood visibly disconcerted. With
an aching spirit he peered at Daisy and demanded:

Tell me, tell me!

Why can't I understand the humans and all the things they do?
Why does none of this big world make sense, and what then
is truly true?

Daisy responded gently and without hesitation:

Is truth a tangible treat to swiftly swallow?
Or a savory scent to forever follow?

Mystery lurks, so hope may surface.
Certitude shirks, so faith may flourish.

A doubting mind, appropriate and perfectly pure.
Forced understanding, a camouflaged and cancerous cure.

Honestly and earnestly wag your tail; honestly and earnestly
make the chase.

Let this be your searching snout's aim; let this be your
trotting paw's pace.

Dennis's whole body fluttered as if he was shaking the water from
his coat after a big ol' bubble bath. He felt . . . lighter. His bliss
contagiously splashed across the crowd.

Fudge

The faithful Frenchie

Fudge, the faithful Frenchie, frolicked forward. His appearance wasn't...
typical. His skin rolls covered his nose holes, exasperating his voice and
making him difficult to understand. Nevertheless, he wheezed out a
question which lay deep on his heart:

I want to be the best friend I can be,
To love the other dogs genuinely.

But sometimes they snarl and growl, sometimes they run away.
How can I love them well if they don't seem to love me?

Daisy gazed into Fudge's earnest eyes. She saw nothing
but virtue and responded in-kind:

Love, ebbing seasons for the soul;
Celestial summer, crucified cold.

An open paw, a gentle jaw.
Be grace for thy fellows' flaw.

Know when to stay, know when to go.
Love takes shape as your knowing grows.

Love cannot control nor connive; Love certainly cannot expect.
But of this I'm sure, Love is the perilous path our souls must trek.

Fudge stared thoughtfully at the ground. He then lifted his snout
and looked at the other dogs. Love coated his eyes. He saw Dewey
the dalmatian appearing distressed. So, Fudge trotted over and softly
nuzzled his head into Dewey's ribcage transmitting a dose of courage to
his new friend.

Dewey

The discouraged Dalmation

Dewey, the discouraged Dalmatian, looked down at Fudge and felt a
newfound fearlessness. He lifted his head and asked Daisy:

Why are my blotches and spots different from most?
The others find me strange, and my stifled spirit shows.

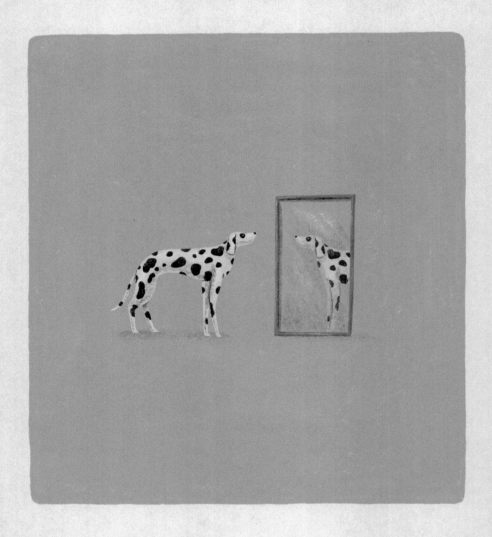

Daisy took one step closer to Dewey investigating his fur coat.
Her eyes welled with compassion. She exclaimed:

Beautiful blotches, stunning spots,
Splendid splotches, dazzling dots.

Gracious gifts, brightly behold,
Holiness dawns where differentness shows.

Your burden's weight, derived by hollow and haunted eyes.
Their palpable blindness invents glossy and glorified lies.

Subversive beauty, an oppressive collar of thickets worn.
Bear their senseless sight, boast thy holy crown of thorns.

Dewey smiled with a smile he hadn't donned since his first crumbs.
He gallivanted back through the crowd with angelic poise.

Coco

The confused Corgi

Coco, the confused Corgi, shuffled forward. She had recently undergone
a procedure by the humans and was truly troubled. She pleaded:

I awoke in pain and on my head was strapped this clunky cone.
Now I can't see or scratch or lick; all I do is moan and groan.

The humans I love so very much, do they truly hate me?
What do I make of such a wretched act of treachery?

Daisy couldn't help but giggle. Not at the question, but because Coco had unknowingly whacked every dog in the crowd with her colossal cone as she walked to center stage. Daisy responded:

Know yourself, you don't, but know yourself, you must.
Impulses ever-present, cunning constancies to trust.

Your owner knows you wholly and can fathom impulses' plague.
The cone thwarts your fated harm, it bars your appetite from being fed.

Is the fence that keeps you home and safe not Love in physical form?
A boundary with a discerning gate, shelter from the storms unknown.

Beloved, bow to Love's beckoning, enjoy their care for now.
For the time will come, as you grow, to venture into stormy clouds.

Coco the conehead straightened her back, she stood dignified. Her cone transformed from a bulky burden into a banner of benevolence.

Howie

The hesitant Hound

Howie, the hesitant Hound, was pacing back and forth, his ears swaying side to side like pendulating pancakes. A decision lay before him, and he was plagued with uncertainty. He rambled with tension in his tone:

A medical alert dog, a therapy pup, or maybe a drug-busting canine.
A hunting dog or maybe a house pup? So many options, so little time.

The countless different paths are vast and terribly overwhelming.
I could do anything, but what should I choose? Please, Daisy, tell me.

In recent years the humans had been offering more and more jobs to dogs. It was a good problem to have, but Daisy didn't covet the weight of such decisions. She responded, optimism permeated her tone:

The choice you make is the choice to choose.
Not choosing anything is the only way to lose.

Fear breeds paralysis, the insidious enemy of a life well-lived.
So, move forward and commit yourself wholly to whatever
path you pick.

What skills have you been given, and what do you desire?
What does the world need, and who do you admire?

Use these questions as a guide
but know the perfect path does not exist.

Life is far more a beautiful experiment
than a target demanding to be hit.

Howie had been taking notes in the dirt with his paw. After committing the questions to memory, he wandered off to find a quiet place to think.

Rosie

The reserved Rottweiler

Rosie, the reserved Rottweiler, rarely made a peep. She possessed the stature of a mighty lioness but the disposition of a shy sheep. With all the courage she could muster, she poked her head out from the crowd and murmured:

I can't be myself around all the others; I'm hiding all the time.
I think if they really knew me, they might not like what they'd find.

I don't know what I'm asking exactly, but I just feel . . . incomplete.
I guess, how can I be the dog that other dogs love when they meet?

Daisy had to turn her ear to hear the muffled mumble.
After a short pause, she tenderly replied:

The dogs might not like you. This is true.
But all dogs have their shadows, including you.

Wounded yet wonderful, broken yet beautiful.
Of one kind. Our shared likeness. Immutable.

All that you are is welcome here, so dig a hole and bury your shame.
Grace licks the blood from our wounds; she summons us out of hiding
by name.

You don't need to be perfect; you don't need to be successful.
Be You. And try your best to become kind, honest, and helpful.

Rosie's eyes were fixed on Daisy alone. Her tongue was partially
sticking out from her slobber-soaked mouth, her fine motor skills
dampened by her focus. After she digested Daisy's words, she awoke
from her daze and looked around at the crowd with a sense of
belonging in her smile.

Annie

The anxious Akita

Annie, the anxious Akita, apprehensively approached the circle. She was trembling and visibly agitated as if a throng of mosquitos were buzzing about her head. But there were no mosquitos. Just a dog and her thoughts. Her erratic eyes fluttered and flickered as she babbled in a whirlwind of emotion:

Behind my steady eyes and in my solid skull lay tumbling
tales of spiraling speculations.
Frantically afoot, my erratic and condemning thoughts
outrun my ability to chase them.

Like a teasing and tormenting tail, these concerns cannot
be caught nor conquered.
Ever-mocking tones of terror, ignited bigger and brighter
the more they're pondered.

Is there rest for a searching soul like mine?
Is peace a place my migrant mind can find?

Daisy didn't hear Annie's questions, she felt them. The weight of the words, the disharmony lurking behind each utterance. Captivated by a sacred sort of solidarity, Daisy replied warmly:

Constructing conceivable realities, the doomed duty of the virtuous.
Your mind's intent pure—to plan for possibilities and
pledge noble purposes.

But swiftly may virtue veer to virulence, left lingering
and lost to its own analysis.
A subtle sinking, your soul's strength sobers to a willing
and weighty weakness.

Irrational as it may seem, the answer is in your paced panting.
A rhythmic remedy, Love's breath, steady and enchanting.

You are here; this is it. No nexts or ifs, no treats to get.
Grace abounds here and now; breathe it in, savor This.

Stillness showered over Annie; a serene silence she'd never heard. Her breath convinced her eyes to close and commanded her body to rest. She laid down, relaxing within the crowd.

Benji

The bubbly Beagle

Benji, the bubbly Beagle, bounced forward. He was a true show dog, slick and swanky. Boasting a bedazzled bandana around his neck, he swaggered right up to Daisy and whispered in her ear:

I paint the truth in little lies, small enough to do no harm.
The praise of others is my prize; I want to love and spread my charm.

So what if I never really caught that rabbit?
Does it truly matter if I didn't literally grab it?

No one gets hurt, and honestly, no one loses.
Is it not noble, the cheer the story produces?

Daisy sighed but surprisingly didn't roll her eyes.

Benevolent yet stern, Daisy put her paw around Benji's shoulders and responded quietly so only he could hear:

Nothing that is has come to be apart from the forming force of words.
Beastly authors of our reality, architects of wondrously wild worlds.

Like gobbling up chocolate crumbs, words can be a savory treat.
But insidious the poison of untamed barking which
lurks within your speech.

Speak only to illustrate what was, what is, or that which ought to be.
All other words flow from a doubting heart unconvinced
of its own dignity.

Raw, real, free of frivolous facades . . . you, my friend, are a beloved prize.
Banish your empty chatter, for it ravages the beauty you've yet to find.

Benji was beguiled by Daisy's words. He felt seen. Giving Daisy a little nuzzle with his nose, he smiled slightly and trotted away to find his humans.

Marvin

The mutable Maltese

Marvin, the mutable Maltese, meandered forward with an uncertainty suffusing his every step. In exasperation he expressed:

I am chasing what I feel, trying to find my way,
But the scent is shifty, changing with every day.

How do I wield all my wants, how do I follow my fickle heart?
How do I get to where I'm going if there's a billion places to start?

Daisy could smell the sweetness of Marvin's sincerity. The question was pure. Daisy's tongue hung in delight, she replied:

Our wants *itch*, our feelings *shed*,
Not all beasts ought to be fed.

But they *kindly* mold us and melt us,
They graciously teach us and tell us.

May we detach and discern, learning to love to listen,
While mindful of the birds and bones vying to blur our vision.

Values forged from eternal virtue illuminate the course to chart.
So follow the mind divinely dancing deeper within your heart.

Marvin's tongue dropped with relief-soaked resonance,
mirroring Daisy's ambient aura.

Wesley

The whiny Whippet

Wesley, the whiny Whippet, stood annoyed. He couldn't believe it had taken this long to finally get a word in. When he felt a little lull, he wailed somewhat dramatically:

I've been dealt a problematic paw, full of such struggle and misery.
The others, they are at fault; they don't know what it's like to be me.

I don't deserve this discomfort. Is there no pity for all my despair?
I want a license to whine and whimper 'til all is just, 'til all is fair.

A few quiet and seemingly unfavorable murmurs spread indistinctly through the crowd. Many of the other dogs knew Wesley. Daisy answered him clearly and directly:

Why do your eyes shift, why does your bark blame?
Pride punishes permanently, like slobber to a flame.

Would anything ever happen, would the future ever take shape,
If we forever floundered in the ripples of another one's wake?

You are a capable creator, an agent for tomorrow's beauty.
Shoulder a worthy purpose and let gratitude be your duty.

If pity is the remedy you so desperately seek,
Courage is the remedy you most certainly need.

Wesley initially took a few steps back, startled and a tad offended by Daisy's frankness. But he saw a glimmer of reassurance streaming from Daisy's eyes.

Lexi

The lackadaisical Lab

Lexi, the lackadaisical Lab, was sprawled out under the next nearest tree. Her eyes were tightly shut but her ears were active and open. Lexi rarely moved an inch, but Daisy's voice vibrated through her bones. She slowly rose and ambled to the crowd more like a turtle than a dog. She warily whispered:

Lounging is my dance, laying my delight.
Must I do more? Or, is this just alright?

Daisy could relate. As she grew in years, slumbering under her sun was all her soul sought. She replied:

To lay when work is required . . . misguided, askew.
To lay as your veritable vocation, noble and true.

Anointed you are to simply be,
Shoulder this lofty cause, do so willingly.

Bear this burden, embody serenity.
Do not lay to lay, lay to love earnestly.

Your guilt is but a hiccup; you work all day long.
Stay the course, and let soulful sleep be your song.

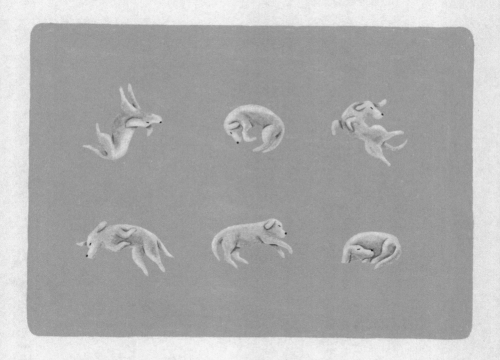

Lexi grinned in delight. She rambled back to her spot under the tree, and with an audible exhale, shamelessly slumped back to sleep.

Pickles

The passionate Pomeranian

Pickles, the petite yet passionate Pomeranian, was prepped and ready.
She spared no pause and promptly posed:

The other dogs wrestled me to the ground and stole my only squeaker.
How do I retaliate with a vengeance even though I'm truly weaker?

A foggy but somber memory coursed through Daisy's mind. She was no stranger to an unwelcome toss-around. Fusing earnest empathy with a tough tenacity, Daisy barked:

One could train with vim and vigor; one could run countless laps.
One could grow their puppy muscles, become strong and fight back.

A noble cause truly worth undertaking,
A noble cause I'm surely not dismissing.

But be wary, for easy the path and dark the fate,
To unwittingly become the very one you hate.

Pernicious power pours from vengeance, a self-induced sort of sickness.
A contented heart knows transcendence, subverting hatred with forgiveness.

Unbeknownst to Daisy, Pickles had already begun working out and had remarkably gained a few pounds of pure Pomeranian muscle in just a couple of weeks. Empowered by Daisy's insight, Pickles continued her training but with radically reformed aspirations.

Watson

The wise Wiener

Watson, the wee and wise Wiener dog, wiggled his way forward. He had spent some time philosophizing and was ready to pose his problem to Daisy. As he wildly wagged his wacky tail, he yelped:

My itsy-bitsy brain can't contain,
My miniature mind, it cannot hold,
All these memories seemingly change,
All these memories, forgotten gold.

I grieve these fleeting moments I can't remember,
Mundane treasures lost in darkness of worlds unknown.
How can I savor my vanished story's splendor?
If I lose my past, can I ever find my soul?

Daisy sat silently and took a moment to think. Watson was wickedly wise for his tiny size. Daisy responded:

Love labors in the menial moments of our past.
Forgotten memories are still treasures that last.

You are You now, beaming and barking, an ever-enduring glory.
Do not hold worry about the boundless details of your fading story.

Love retelling love . . . a higher, wider, deeper drama is brewing.
Self is but the timely expression of Love's endless story renewing.

All these eager tails wagging, do they not wag as one unified soul?
You are but a responsible portion of a far more precious whole.

Watson pensively nodded. Daisy's answer left him satisfied, like the time he covertly devoured a tray of truffles behind the backs of his clueless humans.

Gerald

The genuine German Shepherd

Gerald, the genuine German Shepherd, had been waiting patiently for his turn. He was older than most of the other dogs, as evident by his humble yet dignified presence. With a vulnerable weariness in his voice, the dutiful dog asked:

What must I do to show my humans my love?
Will all of my labor ever be enough?

Daisy had seen Gerald around the park before. He was tireless in his pursuit of excellence; the speed at which he came when called, the sticks and stones he'd spend hours digging up to offer his humans, and how he kindly encouraged all the other pups.

Daisy responded loudly, for all to hear:

A potent power presides in the purity of your very presence.
No work to do, no words to add, simply enjoy Love's essence.

No need to ramble heroically ahead, choking on
the leash of your vain ambitions.
This is not a test to pass, nor a contract
of impossible and countless conditions.

Nor should you, in your shame or fabricated fear,
trot and trail timidly behind.
Rather, learn to walk with your human,
remaining ever enraptured at Love's side.

I tell you, it's not how loud you bark, nor how well you behave.
It's seizing the scandal of grace by seizing the freedom to play.

Gerald jumped with jubilee. He scurried away buoyantly, frolicking
about in the myriad of mud puddles around the park.

Prince

The pompous Pointer

Prince, the pompous Pointer, popped his pointy head above the pack. Prestigiously, as if to prove the legitimacy of his name, he pontificated:

I want my name to last, etched in tags of gold.
I want to be iconic, glorified in legends of old.

As I yearn and yelp for storied splendor,
How do I enjoy the gates I hope to enter?

Daisy's eyes held nothing but charity. Few pups have the guts to
advertise such honest intentions. Daisy answered with an ease of spirit:

> To be remembered, a coveted curse,
> Blurring the lines between last and first.
>
> To be lost in time, the purest of canine callings.
> Weightlessly free, forever, and blissfully falling.
>
> In the losing of oneself, one finds the oneness,
> In being forgotten, one can finally love This.
>
> If you, my friend, can dare to die before you die,
> Your leash will surely snap, and joy will fill your life.

Prince pondered the pill Daisy had placed in his paw, uncertain
if it was something he could swallow. He then left, quietly.
And couldn't be found thereafter.

Mordecai

The morbid Mastiff

Mordecai, the mighty but rather morbid Mastiff, meandered forward. His supreme strength and stately stature had but one vulnerability: his obsessive attention towards his own mortality. He asked the sage in earnest:

Tell us o' wise Daisy, what happens when we die?
And how shall I bear my inevitable end drawing ever nigh?

Daisy resonated with Mordecai. Her days were numbered, and the numbers seemed to be shrinking. A kind of lovely brightness saturated her bark:

I truly do not know, but Hope is no crime.
Maybe we live on; maybe we're lost in time.

Maybe our eyes are opened to color and our tongues unleashed from silence.
Maybe our senses go dark and our bodies dive deep into caves of quiet.

But consider, your appetite is evidence of a satiating source.
Does not your slobbery mouth salivate? So treats exist of course.

Do you long for a truer tale, fields of endless green, cookies forevermore?
Let Hope be your gracious guide, let this life be but a scent of a shinier shore.

The words saturated Mordecai's mind. He looked towards the sky and watched the birds fluttering onward, his spirit adrift with ease.

Gary

The grizzled Golden

Gary, the old and grizzled Golden Retriever, slowly rose, and hobbled towards his dear friend Daisy. Gary and Daisy had grown up together, their humans had once been close companions. They used to wrestle until they could barely breathe. But the days of their youth had passed, and Gary was feeling the loss. With a twinge of heartache in his shaky voice, he asked his Daisy:

Why does the hair on my sniffing snout turn to gray?
Why does everything lovely seem to fade away?

Upon seeing the gray speckles across her beloved friend's snout and hearing his once lively voice quiver, Daisy's head dropped. She wept. Gary comforted her as they shared a moment of symbiotic sorrow. Daisy mustered the fortitude to wipe her tears. She spoke with a passion only age could offer:

Change, a murmured cry . . . the eternal heartbeat of time.
Ruthlessly wondrous, the bonding burden of yours and mine.

May our beauty be our brevity, a love everlasting.
Our souls towed through time with every moon's passing.

Drifting and fleeting, ever repeating,
A song worth singing still leaves us bleeding.

Each new day a new death, so death is but a habit.
Inhale, exhale, stay with your breath, savor it, have it.

A silence fell among the pack. Gary burrowed his head in Daisy's shabby coat as if to say goodbye, and then he stumbled away.

Some of the dogs were huddled together, laying down and crossing paws with each other. Some were sitting upright steadily gazing at Daisy. And some were scattered about, pacing inattentively around the swooping branches of the magnolia tree.

There was nothing more to say.

The mighty sun began to sink deep into the hospitable horizon, staining the sky with puppy belly pinks and panting tongues of red. All the dogs knew their cue and started to scatter, following their humans back to their homes.

All except Dumpster Daisy. She minded the rays recede into darkness. Colors coerced to rest. And then, Daisy drifted into the darkness herself, only to be seen again shimmering in all the other dogs' earnest imitations.

The End

A Note from the Author

Hi!

I'd love to keep writing books and creating art that encourages people to wonder, to see beauty in the world and to love others well.

If you enjoyed The Puppy Prophet, could you take two minutes and give it an honest review on Amazon?

Your support means the world and really will help me keep creating.

Oh, and of course, I'd be honored if you shared the book (#thepuppyprophet) with all your friends, family and that one aunt who loves dogs *way* too much.

Peace and love to you today,

David

Acknowledgments

Thank you to Mila, the dog who inspired this whole creation. I awoke anxious in the middle of the night, my breath a frantic fugitive, the future clawing at my doorstep. Divine intuition sparked, you crawled into my bed and rested your head on my chest. The universe wrapped in fluff, heaven with paws, you are a gift. I'm grateful you'll never read this book; you'd probably laugh at how hard I'm trying to make sense of the world when you seem to do it so naturally.

Thank you to my best friend and forever partner, Emmie. Your love for dogs is unmatched. You know them better than most. I see you in them: kind, loyal, snuggly. Your gracious spirit flows through Daisy's words. You are the greatest gift in my life, I love you.

Thank you to Patrick Atkins for illuminating Daisy's words through your gift of imagery. I couldn't have found a better illustrator, working with you was truly an honor.

Thank you to Brandon O'Neill, for your outpouring of love, support, and wisdom on my creative journey. Your friendship grounds me and fills me with joy.

Thank you to Levi Macallister for your coaching, inspiration, and for a killer foreward.

Thank you to some of my friends: Scottie, Noah, Ben, Hayden, John, Steven C., Nate, Ryan, Cass, Jake R., RJ, Christine, Kendall, Phil, Robin and Jake S., who all, in various capacities, encouraged me spending an inordinate amount of time writing about dogs. Your support makes me want to cry.

Thank you to Luis, Pierre, Martin, Nicole, and Lena. Spending time with you in Peru surrounded by dogs and the magic of the mountains was one of my favorite experiences I've had as a human on this weird planet. Thanks also to Pawsch, Queenie, Grinchie, Angel, and Pato, my Peruvian family of dogs, te amo.

Thank you to Marko and Nevena because your friendship has brought me incalculable joy, a critical element in writing a whimsical book like this.

Thank you to my bucket crew, Nicole, Britney, Morgan, and Val. Love you all. GTB!

Thank you to Melissa and Gerry, how'd I get so lucky with my in-laws?

Thanks to Mom, Dad, Steven, and Tim. Charlie, Amiga and Piper meant so much growing up, I'm so grateful we all got to share life with them. And to the later additions Lindsay, Parker, Boaz, Ronen, and Shiloh. I love you all, thanks for being light in my life.

Thanks to my Greenbriar fam, you all cared for Snow, what an anxiety-ridden experience. Thanks for being family: gracious, supportive, and fun.

Thank you, CJ Goeller, my mentor. Blu will always have a place in my heart and certainly offered some inspiration for Fudge.

Thank you to all my teachers who I don't personally know whose wisdom is scattered throughout these pages: Henri Nouwen, Thomas Merton, Richard Rohr, Thich Nhat Hanh, Scott Erickson, James McCrae, Justin McRoberts, John Mark Comer, Eugene Peterson, Pete Holmes, C.S. Lewis, Jonathan Haidt, Chris Hueretz, Jedidiah Jenkins, Ryan Holiday, Paulo Coehlo, Tim Ferris, Anthony De Mello, Rich Roll, Johann Arnold and, of course, Kahlil Gibran.